Answers!

CELESTA THIESSEN
KEZIAH THIESSEN

CONTENTS

CHAPTER 1 – CAPTURED!

Late in the night, something woke eight-year-old Princess Keziah. She sat up and looked around in the darkness. Her curly brown hair still hung in perfect ringlets. She saw that her brothers, Richard and David, her sisters, Priscilla and Celesta, and her cousins, Mary, Florence, and Conrad, were all still asleep. Keziah and her sisters were triplets. Their cousins had come to the castle for the princesses' birthday party, and then they had stayed for a sleepover. Suddenly, Keziah noticed Nightcat. The huge, gray cat was standing beside her bed. Keziah reached out to pet him and touch his furry wings.

"Nightcat!" she exclaimed. "What are you doing here? I thought your foot was broken."

Nightcat's foot had been injured fighting the dragons that surrounded Kitty Castle. The dragons were very dangerous. The children's parents had gone on a quest to find something to use to fight the dragons, leaving the children with their tutor and cook. Unfortunately, due to a mishap with magic water, their tutor was now a kitten! And no one knew how to change him back.

"I think my foot is better," said Nightcat. "I'm feeling stronger again but I need help."

"What can I do?" asked Keziah.

Keziah heard movement and, soon, five-year-old Prince David joined them. David was her brother. He had brown eyes, just like her sisters and older brother, but David had blonde hair.

"What's happening?" he asked.

"I need help," said Nightcat. "We need to change Mr. Raymond back from a kitten into a person again."

"But how can we do that?" asked David.

"Before I was your cat," explained Nightcat, "I belonged to your Great Aunt Esmeralda. I remember that she had a book about the history of Kitty Castle. I think there might be something in that book that could help Mr. Raymond. Great Aunt Esmeralda called it the 'Book of Answers'."

"Where is the Book of Answers?" asked David.

"In Great Aunt Esmeralda's old home, of course," said Nightcat.

"Outside the walls?!" said Keziah. "But there are dragons out there!"

Their twelve-year old cousin, Mary, was awake now too. She had come over and was staring at Nightcat. Her blue eyes and her mouth were wide open in surprise.

"What's that?" she asked, pointing at their magical pet.

"Nightcat," answered Keziah. "Uhhh...it's kind of hard to explain... If you have a night cat and you treat it kindly and with respect, it will become a magical creature like Nightcat but, if you treat it badly, it will become a dragon."

"What's a night cat?" asked Mary, smoothing her brown hair and trying not to look frightened.

"A night cat is a cat that stays up all night, every night," explained David.

"I think we should wake everyone up," said Nightcat. "We need to find that book."

Just then, they heard a clanging sound coming from down the hall. Keziah and David rushed out to investigate. Nightcat and Mary hurried after them. The sound seemed to be coming from the courtyard. They walked quickly out into the darkness. There were no clouds and the moon was out. Next to a stone bench that leaned against one of the high walls, the children saw a medium-sized, red dragon!

"How did it get into the courtyard?!" gasped David.

"I think it must have dug its way in," said Nightcat, slowly.

"We need to get away from it!" said Keziah.

"Hold on," said Nightcat. "I will put it to sleep with my sparkle breath!"

"What?!" said Mary, looking concerned as she watched Nightcat jump into the sky and fly at the red dragon.

Suddenly, sparkles exploded from Nightcat's open mouth. The dragon dodged and the sparkles flew harmlessly into the castle wall.

The dragon ran quickly and came up behind the children. It opened its large mouth and snagged David by the shirt. Swiftly, it crawled through a hole at the bottom of the castle wall, dragging David with it.

"Oh, no!" cried Mary.

"Quick," shouted Nightcat, "jump on my back!"

Keziah jumped onto Nightcat but Mary stepped back.

"But we're still in our pajamas!" Mary protested.

"Let's go get David!" said Nightcat. "Hurry, Mary, get on."

Carefully, Mary got up onto the big cat's back. Nightcat jumped up into the dark sky. He flapped his powerful wings and flew up and up. The wall was very, very high! Finally, Nightcat reached the top of the castle wall and used his paws to scramble over.

"Wow!" shouted Mary.

Now that they could see past the wall, they spotted the red dragon. It had David in its claws and was starting to fly away.

"Oh, no!" cried Mary.

"Nightcat, you can fly faster!" shouted Keziah.

Nightcat started flying after the red dragon. The dragon had a head start. Nightcat flapped harder. He was gaining on the red dragon. Mary could see her cousin.

"David," called Mary, "we're coming!"

The dragon heard her calling. It turned in the air to face them. As it did so, they got into range. Nightcat blew sparkle dust! The dragon's wings began to move more slowly as it fell asleep. Then it started sinking, spiraling downwards.

"Oh, no!" said Keziah, "David will be crushed underneath the dragon!"

Nightcat swooped down and snatched David out of the dragon's claws just before the dragon hit the dirt. Nightcat landed near the dragon and set David on the ground. David was fast asleep too!

"I think sparkle dust must have gotten on David!" said Keziah.

"It won't be long until he wakes up," said Nightcat.

"Then it probably won't be long until the dragon wakes up?" asked Keziah.

"That's right," said Nightcat. "We'd better get out of here!"

"We're sure a long way from the castle," said Mary.

"And we still have our quest," said Keziah.

"But the good thing is that we are almost at Great Aunt Esmeralda's old house," said Nightcat.

"Let's go!" said Keziah.

"I don't know," said Mary. "Shouldn't we tell the others? They don't know where we are."

"There's no time," said Nightcat. "We need to get Mr. Raymond back to his old self, and we're almost at your Great Aunt Esmeralda's house. Plus I can only carry three on my back at one time, anyway."

Mary and Keziah pulled the sleeping David onto Nightcat with them. Then Nightcat began to fly again. Soon they arrived at a very large, stone house.

"Here it is," said Nightcat.

"Now to search for the book," said Keziah.

"But how will we get in?" asked Mary.

"Nightcat could dig us through, even if the door is locked," said Keziah

"Actually," said Nightcat, "I brought the key." He opened his furry grey paw and there was a small golden key. Nightcat gave the key to Keziah.

Carefully, Mary helped David off Nightcat's back. David was starting to wake up.

"What happened?" he asked, sleepily.

"You got sparkle dust on you!" said Keziah.

"Let's get inside," said Nightcat.

"Before the dragons get us," said David. "Those claws could rip a person in half in one second!"

Keziah took the key up to the large, wooden door. The key fit perfectly. When she turned it, the door creaked open. Following Nightcat, they walked inside.

"There are no lights," said Mary, looking for a light switch.

"I always carry a flashlight with me," said Keziah, taking a flashlight out of her pocket and turning it on.

CHAPTER 2 – THE BOOK OF ANSWERS

"So," said Mary, "where is this book we're looking for?"

"I'm not sure," said Nightcat, "but come in and close the door so dragons don't get in."

Mary pulled the heavy door shut behind her. The house was dark and very old, with dust and rubble everywhere.

"I think I have an idea where it might be," said Nightcat. "I think it's in a golden chest that's locked with the same key that opens the door."

"Where's the golden chest?" asked Mary.

"We'll have to search for it," said Nightcat.

They started walking.

"This might be a little dangerous so we will have to stick together," said Keziah.

"Well, I think we're going in the right direction," Nightcat said, as he tried to remember the layout of Great Aunt Esmeralda's house.

Suddenly, Mary stopped. "Am I imagining things? Do you see, under that large stone, a glint of gold?"

"I do," cried David, rushing forward. The house seemed to shake a little.

"Quiet..." hushed Nightcat. "Loud noised could cause an old and unstable house like this to fall down."

"This is it!" said David in an excited whisper. "But I can't get it out."

"I think Nightcat could lift the stone away," said Keziah. Nightcat got ready. He put his head under the stone and pushed it up onto his shoulders. The stone slowly shifted.

Keziah walked forward and tried to lift the golden box. She groaned.

"I can't lift it!"

Mary and David rushed forward to help her.

"Just a minute," said Nightcat. "I can help you." He finished moving the stone and, together, the children lifted the box out.

"The key will unlock the box but I'm not sure we want to unlock it now," said Keziah.

"You're right," said Nightcat. "We should wait until we're back in Kitty Castle."

"Yeah, we don't want those mean dragons to steal the book," added David.

"Uh oh!" said Mary.

"What?" asked Keziah.

"Dragon!"

"Right in front of us!" said Keziah, who had followed Mary's gaze.

There, before them, stood a very large, brown dragon!

"Get behind me!" shouted Nightcat.

The children ducked behind their huge cat as he took a deep breath. Then Nightcat blew sparkle dust at the large dragon. The sparkle dust twinkled in the darkness.

The dragon fell to the floor with a thump! It was fast asleep.

"That was a close one!" said David.

"Now," said Nightcat, "we had better get out of here before more dragons come."

Together, Mary, Keziah, and David lifted the golden box onto Nightcat's back. Then they followed their furry friend out of the old house.

"Umm..." said Keziah, after they were out, "how will we get back to Kitty Castle?"

"On my back, of course," said Nightcat. "I am very strong. I can carry this box *and* all of you."

"Are you sure there's room?" asked Mary.

"There will have to be," said David. "I'm not staying here or walking back!"

The children crowded up onto Nightcat's back, along with the large golden box.

"Giddy up!" said David.

Keziah and Mary giggled. Nightcat tried not to feel insulted as he pumped his powerful wings and lifted off the ground.

When they arrived back at the castle, it was early morning. The other children were only just waking up.

"Where were you?" asked Richard.

"We found Great Aunt Esmeralda's history book!" said Mary.

"What's that?!" cried their cousin, Conrad.

"It's the Book of Answers," said Keziah, impatiently.

"No...that!" said Florence, pointing toward Nightcat.

"That's our pet," said David, proudly.

"Where did you find the book?" asked Celesta, ignoring her cousins' outbursts.

"In her house, of course," said Keziah.

"You went outside?!" asked Richard.

"I got captured by a dragon!" said David.

"What!?" cried the other children at the same time.

"It's okay now," said Nightcat. "Let's look at what we found. Richard, please take the golden box off my back. It's getting heavy."

Richard placed the golden chest on the floor.

"How do we open it?" Richard asked.

"I have the key!" said Keziah. Carefully, she put the key into the lock.

"Wait!" said Richard, suddenly. "I don't know if opening the box is a good idea. Are you sure it's safe?"

"If the key opens it, it's safe," Keziah reassured Richard.

"How do you know?" he asked.

"Aunt Esmeralda wouldn't put something dangerous in her box, would she?" said Keziah.

"Let's just open it and see," said Celesta.

"I need help turning this old key," said Keziah, struggling to turn it. "I think the lock's rusty."

"Here," said Richard, "let me try."

Richard took the key and turned it in the lock. The golden box clicked open. Cautiously, Richard lifted the lid. Keziah reached inside and took out a very old, dusty book.

"That doesn't look very special," said their cousin, Florence.

"It's not the book," said Nightcat. "It's what's inside."

"Okay," Keziah explained to her cousins, "here's the situation. We accidentally turned our tutor, Mr. Raymond, into a kitten. He's one of the kittens you saw downstairs yesterday."

"How did you change your tutor into a cat?" asked Florence.

"Richard splashed him with the magic water," said David.

"It was an accident," explained Richard.

"Some dragons got into the castle," said Keziah. "Richard missed the dragons and splashed Mr. Raymond with the water instead."

"Magic cats and magic water?!" exclaimed Florence. "This really is *too* much!"

"It's okay," said Priscilla. "You'll get use to it."

"Now let's find out how to turn him back!" said Nightcat.

CHAPTER 3 – GOOD NEWS AND BAD NEWS

Keziah opened the book. She gasped. "How are we going to find out how to turn Mr. Raymond back? This book isn't in English!"

"What language is it?" asked Mary.

"I don't know," said Keziah.

"Let me see," said Priscilla. "Hmmm...too bad Mr. Raymond can't translate it for us."

"What do you think?" Celesta asked Nightcat.

"I can't read," Nightcat said sadly. "Richard," said Nightcat, "haven't you studied different languages? Maybe you can read it?" He nudged the book toward Richard.

The older prince looked carefully at the book.

"No, I've never seen that kind of writing before."

"I know," said David, "we can just look at the pictures."

"Well," Keziah said, flipping through the pages, "here's a picture of the unicorn that Priscilla for her birthday."

The other children pressed in closer to see.

"Its horn is sparkling," said Priscilla.

"It's being dipped into a bucket of water," said David.

"The background looks like it's in the room under the castle, where the pool of magic water is," said Keziah.

"Hey," said Richard, staring at the writing in disbelief. "I think the writing is turning into English!"

"It's my bracelet!" exclaimed Celesta. "Look!" As she brought her gold and blue bracelet closer to the page, the words became readable, but when she took her bracelet away, they looked strange again!

"Celesta, hold your bracelet close to the page and let's read it!" said Keziah.

"It says that the diamond horn of the unicorn will change the water into reverse. So whatever change the water made, it will be undone," said Richard.

"We mustn't dip the unicorn's horn into the whole pool!" said Priscilla.

"No," said Nightcat, gravely, "or we will have no more magic water with which to fight the dragons."

"We can dip it into a bucket of water, like the picture shows," suggested Keziah.

The children looked at the book and talked about it excitedly.

"Shhh..." said Keziah, suddenly. She looked at Nightcat. "Nightcat," she said, "I need to talk to you alone."

The other children looked at her oddly as Nightcat led the way into one of the other rooms.

"What?" he asked her.

"This is getting more and more dangerous. If dragons can dig through stone and burn almost anything, how are we going to stay safe? What if they get into the castle again?"

Keziah was scared. She stood close to Nightcat and looked at her old friend.

"Hmmm..." said Nightcat, "I'm not sure. All we can do is our best. I will try to protect you, and I know your brothers and sisters and your cousins will too – we will all protect one another."

"You're right," said Keziah, sighing. "I'm just getting tired of fighting the dragons all the time. Nothing feels safe anymore."

Nightcat rubbed up against her with his huge head and purred loudly. She patted him between his large, furry gray ears. Then they went back to the other children.

"Now," said Nightcat, "it's time to turn Mr. Raymond back into Mr. Raymond."

The children crowded eagerly around Nightcat.

"I'll get a bucket and then I'll get some water from the secret passageway," said Richard. "I think I should be the one to do it."

"Just don't miss this time!" said David.

The other children laughed.

Richard left to get the bucket and the magic water.

"I'll get my unicorn," said Priscilla.

"I'll get the kitten that is Mr. Raymond," said Keziah.

"I'll come with you," said Celesta, joining her as they walked down to the kitchen.

The other children waited in their room.

When Celesta and Keziah reached the kitchen, they saw two kittens sleeping by the fire. The black and white kitten was Sushi. The grey and white kitten was Surprise. The little orange kitten, who was Mr. Raymond, was nowhere to be seen!

"Oh, no!" said Celesta. "Where is Mr. Raymond?"

"Daisy!" cried Keziah.

Their startled cook came sleepily from her room.

"What is it?" she asked.

"Mr. Raymond isn't here!" said Keziah.

"He must be around here somewhere! I left him right here with the other kittens," said Daisy.

Keziah, Celesta, and Daisy searched the kitchen. The little orange kitten was not there!

"We'll have to search the castle," said Daisy. "Tell the other children. Mr. Raymond must be found!"

"Wait," said Keziah. "What if he got into one of the passageways?"

"Let's leave the searching of the passageways to Nightcat," suggested Celesta.

"Good idea," said Daisy. "We don't want your cousins getting lost."

So Celesta and Keziah went back upstairs to tell the others.

"Where's Mr. Raymond?" cried David, before they could speak.

"He's lost!" said Keziah.

"We'll need to search for him," said Celesta.

"Nightcat," said Keziah, "could you search the passageways to see if he's there?"

"Certainly," said their large pet. Nightcat left quietly to begin his search.

"Come on, everyone," said Celesta. "Let's start looking!"

So the children began to search the castle for one small orange kitten.

"Mr. Raymond! Here Mr. Raymond!" their cousins called.

"I have an idea," said Keziah.

"What?" asked David.

"Cat treats!" Keziah exclaimed.

"That *is* a good idea," said Celesta. "Let's go see if Daisy has any."

Celesta and Keziah walked down the stairs to the kitchen. The other children continued to search in the library. The girls found the cook still looking around in the kitchen.

"He just must be here somewhere," Daisy muttered.

"Daisy," Keziah said, "do you have any cat treats?"

"Cat treats!" exclaimed Daisy. "Why didn't I think of that?" She looked in the pantry and pulled out an extra large bag of kitty treats. "I baked these treats myself," their cook said.

Celesta took the bag from her and shook it. The two kittens by the fireplace looked up at once. She shook the bag again.

"Cat food!" said Celesta. Both kittens came quickly to Celesta. "It works!" she exclaimed.

"I think you should give some treats to the kittens," Keziah said. "We shouldn't tease them."

"You're right!" said Celesta. She pulled two treats out of the bag and gave them to the kittens. "We don't want to be mean to these little night cats." The kittens ate the treats and rubbed against the princess' legs. Celesta walked up the stairs to the library, shaking the bag. The little kittens tried to follow.

"No, no," said Daisy. "We don't want the two of you getting lost too!" She shut the door to keep the kittens in the kitchen.

Keziah and Celesta entered the library, shaking the treat bag.

"Food!" called Celesta.

"I don't think he's in the library," said Priscilla.

"We've looked everywhere!" grumbled David.

CHAPTER 4 – IN THE HOLE

"We haven't looked everywhere or we would have found him," said Celesta. "He couldn't get out of the castle or just disappear."

"We didn't look in the courtyard," said Keziah.

Celesta, Keziah, and David walked down the stairs and out into the courtyard.

Once they were outside, Keziah pointed to the garden. "Look! Our plants are starting to grow."

The children looked at their garden. They could see little green shoots coming up from the dirt.

"I can't believe our plants are growing already," said Keziah.

Then David pointed to the wall. "We didn't fix the hole under the castle wall!"

"Oh, no!" said Celesta. "Do you think Mr. Raymond could have gone down there?"

"I don't know," said David, peering into the dark hole. The castle wall was very thick. "I think I should check. It's the only way we'll know for sure."

"No," said Celesta. "Don't do it! It's too dangerous."

"I'll just take a quick look," said David. "We have to find out."

David dashed down into the hole before Celesta could stop him. In less than one minute, he came back, holding something in his hands.

"Mr. Raymond wasn't down there," he said, "but look what I found!" In his hands was a golden flute!

"David! You just found your special thing!" cried Celesta.

"I can keep it?" asked David.

"You found it," said Keziah. "You get to keep it!"

"All right!" said David. "This is awesome! I don't care that you princesses each got two things, because this is way better!"

"We better get that hole fixed," said Keziah.

"Let's go ask Daisy and our cousins to help us patch up this hole before more dragons get in," said Celesta.

"Right," said David, "and we'd better hurry."

The children ran into the castle. They found Daisy in the kitchen, still calling for Mr. Raymond. "Mr. Raymond! Come here, Kitty!"

"Daisy, can you help us? There's a hole under the courtyard wall and we need to fix it," said Celesta.

"Oh, no! Show me where."

"I'll go upstairs and get our cousins to help," said Keziah, putting the cat treats down.

Their cook closed the kitchen door, to keep the two kittens inside. Daisy, Celesta, and David got some shovels and went out into the courtyard. There was a pile of bricks and dirt near the hole.

"How are we going to glue the bricks together?" asked David.

Just then, Keziah and the cousins arrived in the courtyard.

"Let's just fill the hole in and then we'll pour some cement in on top," said Daisy.

"Good idea," said Celesta.

"Yeah," said David. "I guess using our glue sticks wouldn't have worked."

All the other children laughed.

"This will be good. The dragons won't be able to dig back through so easily," said Keziah.

The seven of them started to shovel the dirt and bricks into the hole.

Meanwhile, Nightcat was searching the labyrinth under the Kitty Castle.

He was calling, "Meow, meow, meow, meow," which means 'Mr. Raymond' in cat. It was very dark in the passage, but kittens and cats can see in the dark. Nightcat was starting to feel discouraged. Then a thought came to him. *I wonder if Mr. Raymond got lost in the same place he did the last time he went into the labyrinth.*

Back out in the courtyard, the hole was half filled in.

"This is sure taking a long time," said Florence.

Suddenly, Conrad slipped right down into the hole. "Ahh!!!" His feet sank down into the loose dirt that they had just shoveled into the hole.

"Help me!" he cried.

Daisy tried to grab hold of Conrad but he was too far down in the hole.

"Help! The dragons are going to get me! They will eat my feet!"

"There is dirt under your feet," explained Celesta. "The dragons won't get you."

Daisy said, "Maybe if I lower one of you down there, you'll be able to reach him."

"Good idea," said Keziah.

"I'll go down," said Mary. "I'm the biggest, so I'll be able to pull him up."

Carefully, Daisy lowered Mary into the hole. She easily reached her brother, and Daisy pulled them both out.

"Thank you!" said Conrad. "You saved my life!"

"Let's get this finished before someone else slides in," said Mary.

Soon all the dirt and bricks were in the hole.

"Mary, help me get the cement," said Daisy. In a few minutes, they returned with a wheelbarrow full of cement.

Just then, Richard and Priscilla came into the courtyard.

Priscilla looked at their garden. "I can't believe our plants are already growing!"

"Richard," said Daisy, "you can pour the cement into the hole. It's very heavy."

"Okay." Richard poured the cement over the opening of the hole. Then he smoothed it with a shovel.

"We were wondering what was taking you so long," said Priscilla.

"I was wondering the same thing about you!" said Keziah.

Finally, their work was done.

"I hope Nightcat has had better luck finding Mr. Raymond than we have," said Keziah. "We've been working on this almost the whole time."

"Let's go check in the library again. Maybe Mr. Raymond has wandered back there by now," said Celesta.

Tiredly, the children walked back into the castle. They put the shovels away. Keziah grabbed the bag of cat treats from the kitchen and began to shake it again.

They walked up to the library and looked around.

"Nightcat's not here. I hope he didn't get lost," said David.

Keziah laughed. "Nightcat wouldn't get lost. He can see in the dark and he knows the passageways very well."

CHAPTER 5 –WHAT NONSENSE!

"I know; let's check in our playroom," suggested Celesta.

They went up the stairs. Keziah shook the bag of cat treats.

"Food!" she called. They didn't find the small orange kitten in their playroom either.

"Where could he be?" asked Mary.

The children walked slowly back to the library.

When they got there, they heard a loud, creaking noise. The secret passageway was opening! It was Nightcat! He had a small orange kitten in his mouth. Nightcat was carrying Mr. Raymond just like a mother cat would carry her kitten!

"Nightcat!" cried Priscilla. "You found him!"

"Did you find him where he got lost last time?" asked Keziah.

Nightcat carefully put the kitten down.

"Yes, in the same place!" Nightcat looked eagerly at the bag in Celesta's hand. "Could I have a cat treat?" he asked.

"Sure," said Keziah, grabbing a treat out of the bag. "This one looks just like you!"

Celesta looked at the treat and saw that it was true! Daisy had baked the cat treats, and some of them were in the shape of Nightcat!

"I'm eating me!" Nightcat giggled.

Mr. Raymond meowed so Keziah gave him a treat as well.

"We had better change Mr. Raymond back now," said Richard. "We have everything ready in our bedroom."

"Let's do it!" said Priscilla, scooping the little kitten up into her arms.

"Remember," said David to Richard, as they walked back to the room, "don't miss!"

When they got back to their bedroom, Richard took the kitten from Priscilla.

"Dip the unicorn's horn into this bucket of water," he said.

"Don't miss!" David said again.

"Shhh..." hushed Celesta.

Priscilla took her small unicorn statue from her dresser. She brought it over to the bucket of water. Slowly, she dipped its horn into the water. A bright, white light came from the diamond on the tip of the horn.

"I think it's working," said Mary.

Richard dunked the small kitten right into the water!

Splash!

Suddenly, there was Mr. Raymond, with his foot stuck in the pail of water! Quickly, Nightcat began to shrink into his daytime form.

"What!?" exclaimed Mr. Raymond. "What have you children done?" he shouted.

Down in the kitchen, Daisy heard shouting coming from upstairs. When she got to the children's bedroom, she saw that Mr. Raymond was back! And he was standing in a bucket of water!

"I demand to know what has happened here," said Mr. Raymond. He looked at Daisy. "What have you let the children do?!"

"Me?" squawked Daisy. "I didn't *let* them *do* anything!"

"Why is my foot in a pail of water?!" he demanded.

"Don't you remember anything?" asked Richard.

"Of course," said Mr. Raymond. "I have an excellent memory."

"Do you remember that you were a kitten?" asked David.

"What nonsense!" cried Mr. Raymond.

"Do you remember that the dragons got into the castle?" asked Richard.

"You children have been very naughty," said Mr. Raymond. "I think it's time for your cousins to go home."

The children all looked at each other and raised their eyebrows. Mr. Raymond didn't remember anything that had happened!

"It's daytime now," said Daisy. "I think it would be safe for your cousins to go home...but I think all of you should get dressed first!"

The children looked at each other and giggled. They were still wearing their pajamas! The children got dressed and Mr. Raymond went to get dry socks.

After all the children had changed out of their pajamas, they met back in the children's bedroom.

"I'm going to work on my Science homework," announced Keziah. "I'm getting behind on it."

"Say goodbye to your cousins first," replied Daisy.

The children walked down to the front door.

"Goodbye," said Mary. "It has been a very fine adventure."

"Goodbye," said Keziah. "We may never see you again."

"Yes," said Mary, "travel is getting very dangerous."

"I hope we will soon be rid of these dragons," said Conrad.

"Yes," said Richard. "We will work toward that, with Nightcat's help, of course."

They gave each other a goodbye hug. Then Mary, Florence, and Conrad slipped quietly out the front door. Daisy fastened the latch behind them.

The children walked up the stairs towards the library, where they would work on their homework.

"Do you think Mr. Raymond will ever believe in the dragons and Nightcat?" asked David.

"I think it will take a loooooonnnnnnng time," said Keziah.

"Do you think Mom and Dad will get home soon?" asked Priscilla.

Richard simply shook his head.

"I think they might be gone a very long time," said Celesta.

"At least we have Nightcat," said Keziah.

As they walked into the library, they saw little Nightcat sleeping in his favorite spot by the window. The children patted him gently and listened to his familiar purring.

KITTY CASTLE BOOKS

Get all the Kitty Castle books on Amazon.com!

KITTY CASTLE 1 - NIGHTCAT

KITTY CASTLE 2 - SURPRISES!

KITTY CASTLE 3 - ANSWERS!

KITTY CASTLE 4 - MYSTERY!

KITTY CASTLE 5 – REUNION

KITTY CASTLE 6 - CELEBRATIONS

If you liked this book, please leave us a great review on Amazon.com! Thanks for reading!

Bruce County Public Library
1243 Mackenzie Rd.
Port Elgin ON N0H 2C6

CPSIA information can be obtained at www.ICGtesting.com
Printed in the USA
LVOW07s0047050915

452957LV00001B/15/P